To Sherre—who has a heart full
of love and a head full of ideas,
some of which have overflowed
onto these pages.   —L. S.

To my father   — C. B. S.

MONKEY SOUP

by Louis Sachar

illustrations by Cat Bowman Smith

Alfred A. Knopf 🐆 New York

My daddy is sick in bed.

He can blow his nose louder than anyone in the world. I wish I could blow my nose that loud.

Mommy is making him chicken soup. She says that will make him feel better.

I'm making him soup too. I put Band-Aids in my
soup. Band-Aids always make *me* feel better.

Mommy adds carrots to her soup. I add balloons to
my soup. Balloons make me happy.

When daddy is sick, his face turns pale. He needs more color in his face. So I put crayons in the soup too.

Monkey is helping me.

Monkey says, "Oooh-ooh, eeeee-eeee, ahhhh-ahhh." Daddy taught him to say that. Monkey wants Daddy to feel better too.

Daddy's door is closed, but I can still hear him
sneeze. We'd better put tissues in the soup, Monkey.

I'll put my blanket in the soup to keep Daddy warm.

Grandma gave me this shirt. It has lots of buttons.
The buttons will make the soup taste delicious.

Bubbles make me laugh. Daddy blows big bubbles,
and I try to pop them. Poor Daddy can't blow bubbles
today. I'll pour them into the soup.

I wash my hands before I eat. I brush my teeth after
I eat. Daddy shouldn't get out of bed, so I'll put a bar
of soap and my toothbrush in the soup.

I put a napkin in the soup so in case it spills, it won't make a mess.

What else?

Monkey wants to go in the soup too!

Mommy stirs her chicken soup with a big wooden spoon. I stir my Monkey soup with my horse.

I take it to Daddy. I hope he likes it.

Have some Monkey soup, Daddy. It's good for you.
It will make you feel all better.

Daddy likes it. "Delicious!" he says. "I feel all better."

Bless you, Daddy.

THIS IS A BORZOI BOOK PUBLISHED BY ALFRED A. KNOPF, INC.

Text copyright © 1992 by Louis Sachar
Illustrations copyright © 1992 by Cat Bowman Smith
All rights reserved under International and Pan-American Copyright
Conventions. Published in the United States by Alfred A. Knopf, Inc.,
New York, and simultaneously in Canada by Random House of Canada
Limited, Toronto. Distributed by Random House, Inc., New York.

Library of Congress Cataloging-in-Publication Data
Sachar, Louis, 1954–
Monkey soup / by Louis Sachar : illustrated by Cat Bowman Smith.
p.   cm. Summary: With the help of her toy monkey, a girl
prepares an all-encompassing soup full of Band-Aids,
crayons, and tissues for her father who is sick in bed.
ISBN 0-679-80297-5 (trade) – ISBN 0-679-90297-X (lib. bdg.)
[1. Sick–Fiction. 2. Monkeys–Fiction. 3. Toys–Fiction.]
I. Smith, Cat Bowman, ill.   II. Title.   PZ7.S1185Mo 1992
[E]–dc20   91-15858

2   4   6   8   0   9   7   5   3   1
Manufactured in Singapore